To my parents, for their unconditional love, endless dedication, and for being the best role models. Amo vocês! — J.P.

For Hugo — C.C.

PEIXARIA

Printed in China 38 • First edition, November 2021 • Book design by Rae Crawford • The text type was set in Atma. The display type was set in Bigelow Rules. • The illustrations were created digitally, using Procreate and Adobe Photoshop.

BiSa'S CaRNavaL

by Joana PaStRo

illuStRaTeD by CaRolina CoRoa

Orchard Books
An Imprint of Scholastic Inc. · New York

Under a rainbow-bannered sky,
trumpets, trombones, tubas,
and saxophones sing

Louder, Faster,
Faster, Louder!
It's CARNAVAL!

"Carnaval has always been my favorite holiday. See, Clara? I was your age in this one." Bisa points to a faded picture.

"You look just like me!" I turn the page, excited to see all the colorful costumes.

"You're in every picture! With Biso and Grandpa, with Mom and Aunt Maria . . . I remember this one! We were cats. Meow meow!"

"We were tigers!" Bisa tickles my tummy.

"This year, I want the best fantasia ever!"
My brain swirls with ideas.
"Of course!" Bisa counts the coins from her special coffee can.
A clank, clunk, clink, like the maracatu call.
"Vamos lá!" Bisa says.

We shop for a big bolt of fabric,
big enough to sew fantasias
for my cousins, my sisters, and me.
We pick the prettiest pattern.
One that screams tropical dreams,
as bold and bright as a summer day.

OFERTAS

Bisa prefers the prettiest price tag.
One that whispers there will be money left.
"Lindo!" she says. *Beautiful!*

LINHAS

Through narrow cobblestone streets and
between vibrant walls,
the salty, sticky ocean breeze follows us
up, down, and behind the slopes.
"Eu amo Carnaval!" I sing and prance all the way home.
I love Carnaval!

"We all do," Bisa says.
"Oh Bisa, why can't you come?" we ask.
She laughs. "Carnaval won't wait for old legs. You'll enjoy it for me."

Back home, we help gather supplies.
We search desks, dressers, and drawers,

and scavenge the streets for
anything sparkly, colorful, and fun.

Fabric, scissors, thread, and glue.
Sequins, buttons, and last year's tulle.
Bisa's sewing machine hums to life.

Tchuk, tchuk, tchuk.
Snip, snip, snip.
Zig, zag, zig.

"Can I help?"
Bisa teaches me how to sew the buttons.
Through and through. Nice and tight.
In a few days, she whips up
uma, duas, três fantasias.
Four, five, six, seven, eight.

Bisa adds final touches. A feather here,
a ribbon there.
We slip into our fantasias.
Flowers, tiaras, and cat ears, too!
Our faces beam a kaleidoscope of colors.

Around the room we dance and
sprinkle extra glitter.
Purpurina, everywhere!
We look *fabulous.*
Our spirits are high, our hearts are full!
This is Carnaval!

Popcorn and ice cream fuel us up.
In front of Bisa's house, the parade bounces by,
followed by hundreds of happy faces.
Faces that, for a few days, forget their troubles.

PIPOCA

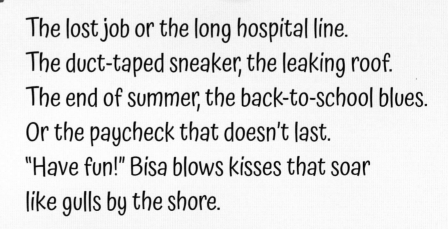

The lost job or the long hospital line.
The duct-taped sneaker, the leaking roof.
The end of summer, the back-to-school blues.
Or the paycheck that doesn't last.
"Have fun!" Bisa blows kisses that soar
like gulls by the shore.

The music pulls us in.
WE sing,
      jump,
            dance,
arms and hands in the air, following the crowd.

Confete showers enchant and serpentina spirals bedazzle.
We mingle with beauty queens, super heroes, fairies,
harlequins, and people from all over the world.
Different accents, cultures, beliefs.

Frevo dancers swivel their umbrellas in the air.
Side to side, forward and back.
Frantic and feverish, like the ground is boiling hot.
But something is missing.

For a moment, I close my eyes.
I take in the brass band and scents galore.
Sweet, sour, citric. Like goiabada, carambolas, pitangas.
They surround me in a warm embrace,
just like my bisa's, and suddenly I know.

Someone is missing . . .

"If Bisa can't come to Carnaval,
we'll bring Carnaval to Bisa!" I say.
All it takes is a little detour.
I blow my whistle, leading the way . . .

All are welcome!

... and I open the door, making way for musicians, dancers, giant dolls, and all those happy faces.

Bisa's laughter is as contagious as
Carnaval fever.
We rush into her arms and . . .
our hearts go BOOM!

LOUDER,
FASTER,
FASTER,
LOUDER!

AUTHOR'S NOTE

Writing this story brought back many happy memories of watching my mom sitting at her sewing machine as she made my costume for the festival. One year, I entered a costume contest, and even though I knew I didn't stand a chance of winning, I didn't care. It was Carnaval!

Growing up in Brazil means that as soon as January rolls around, preparations begin. The excitement grows and grows until it finally erupts into the extravagant festival of Carnaval that the whole world admires. Carnaval is a time of celebration leading up to the more quiet time of Lent, the Christian time of reflection, and many countries have their own traditions, including the United States. In New Orleans, revelers wear masks and pass around beads for Mardi Gras, or "Fat Tuesday."

Street Carnaval is common in all of Brazil, but each region celebrates a little differently. Clara and Bisa live in Olinda, a seaside city in the northeast where frevo is a trademark dance. Playing off the word "fervo," or "I boil," performers and parade-goers carry small umbrellas while they move, making it look like their feet barely touch the ground. Giant dolls, another Carnaval mainstay in Olinda, are made out of papier-mâché and fabric by local artists. At fifteen feet tall, they are quite the spectacle!

The true beauty of Carnaval rests in its power to bring people together. All are welcome to participate in the parade, and for several days we are unified in our joy. Carnaval is a celebration about being creative, spontaneous, and surrounded by loved ones.

Just like Clara and Bisa.

ILLUSTRATOR'S NOTE

Clara's story immediately brought me back to my childhood. My bisa moved from Rio de Janiero to the north, where I was born, but she always reminisced about the glamour and joy of being carioca at this special time of the year. Carnaval is such a special and joyous time, and it was great fun revisiting childhood memories with my sisters as I began to sketch and eventually add color to this vibrant story.

It was Joana's words that helped transport me back into the heart of a child as I began to bring this world — our beautiful Brazil — to life. Even though I am far from my home country, the spirit of the holiday has never left me, and I hope you feel it in the pages of this book.

GLOSSARY*

bisa (BEE-zah): short for bisavó, great-grandma

biso (BEE-zoh): short for bisavô, great-grandpa

uma (OO-mah): one

duas (DOO-ahs): two

três (TREHS): three

confete (kohn-FEH-chee): confetti

maracatu (mah-rah-kah-TOO): dance and music typical of the state of Pernambuco in Brazil

fantasia (fuhn-tah-ZEE-ah): costume

purpurina (poor-poo-REE-nah): glitter

serpentina (sehr-pehn-TEE-nah): streamer

*These are only some of the words found in Clara's story. If there are others you'd like to learn, you can find them in a Brazilian Portuguese/English dictionary!